Sleeping Beauty

Princess Stories Starring Aurora

Adapted by Wendy Wax and Rita Balducci
Illustrated by Disney Storybook Artists

CONTENTS

Reader's Digest
Children's Books

Pleasantville, New York • Montréal, Québec • Bath, United Kingdom

Sleeping Beauty

*O*nce upon a time, there was a king named Stefan. When King Stefan's daughter, Aurora, was born, he invited everyone in the kingdom to join him in a great feast to celebrate the happy occasion. King Hubert and his young son, Phillip, were among the guests, for it had already been decided that Phillip and Aurora would marry someday.

Three good fairies named Flora, Fauna, and Merryweather were also invited, and they came with gifts for the child. Flora gave the baby the gift of beauty. Fauna gave the child the gift of song. But before Merryweather could give her gift, the evil fairy Maleficent

DISK 1

I

appeared. She was angry she had not been invited, so she put a curse on the baby. "Before the sun sets on her sixteenth birthday," Maleficent declared, "she will prick her finger on the spindle of a spinning wheel...and die!"

Maleficent's power was so strong that neither Flora, Fauna, nor Merryweather could completely undo the curse. But because Merryweather had not yet given her gift, she was able to change the curse. Instead of dying, the princess would fall asleep and remain that way until she received a kiss from her true love.

To protect Aurora, the fairies took her to a cottage in the woods where they lovingly raised her. So no one would know who she was, the fairies changed her name to Briar Rose.

Briar Rose grew up not knowing she was a princess, but she was beautiful and good. On her sixteenth birthday, the fairies sent her out to pick berries so they could make her a special dress. Briar Rose happily obeyed her dear friends.

3

4

As Briar Rose walked through the woods, she began to sing a love song. Her voice was so beautiful that all the woodland animals gathered to listen. A young man on horseback heard the singing, too, and he rode toward the sweet-sounding voice. He was enchanted by Briar Rose's song and he began to sing along with her. At first, she was startled to see the young man and hear his strong voice joining with her own. He seemed like a prince out of one of her dreams. She was captivated by the young man. They danced together as they sang, and by the end of the duet, the two young people had fallen deeply in love.

5

6

7

When Briar Rose arrived back at the
cottage, she breathlessly told the fairies
that she had fallen in love with a young
man in the woods. It was then that the
fairies had to tell her the truth about her
birth and her name. She was heartbroken
to learn that she was truly a princess, and
was already betrothed to Prince Phillip.
With a heavy heart, Aurora walked with
the fairies back to her father's castle.

Aurora was home at last, but her mind
was on her true love. Suddenly, a strange
green light caught her eye. She followed
the light all the way to the tallest tower in

DISK 2

9

the castle, where a spinning wheel glowed in the corner. The fairies realized Aurora was in danger, and they raced to stop her from touching the spinning wheel. But before they could stop her, Aurora pricked her finger on the spindle. She instantly fell to the floor and lay motionless.

The fairies laid Aurora gently on her bed. "The king and queen will be heartbroken," they said. "To save them from this

10

heartache, we must put everyone else in the kingdom to sleep."

At the very same time, the
young man with whom Aurora
had fallen in love came to the
cottage looking for her. Instead
11 he met the evil Maleficent.
Maleficent knew the young man
was really Prince Phillip, and she
quickly chained him in her dungeon.

The good fairies soon discovered his
12 true identity and came to his rescue. They
freed the prince and gave him a magic
sword and shield to fight Maleficent.
Prince Phillip slashed his way through the
13 brambles surrounding the castle.
Maleficent turned herself into a huge
dragon and set fire to the brambles.

Prince Phillip bravely fought the
14 dragon, using his sword to kill the evil
creature. Then he raced to Aurora's side and
kissed her. The spell was
broken! Aurora's eyes
15 opened to see the face
of the young man she
loved, and all over the
kingdom, everyone
else awoke, too. The
16 fairies were overjoyed
as the happy pair
joined hands. True love
had conquered all!

Sleeping Beauty

Aurora in: A Dream Come True

Princess Aurora had never been so happy in her life. She was about to marry Prince Phillip, the dearest, most handsome man she had ever met, and the man who had been promised to her since the day she was born. Prince Phillip also happened to be the man of her dreams—really! She remembered the day in the forest when they first met....

Aurora had been singing to her animal friends about her dream of falling in love with a handsome stranger. Prince Phillip, who happened to be nearby, was enchanted by her angelic voice and set off to find her. As soon as Aurora and Phillip looked into each other's eyes, they felt as if they'd known each other forever. It was true love.

Play
Song
3

"Princess Aurora!" said the courtier, calling her back to the present. "I'm afraid I need you to go over the list for your engagement party."

"Oh!" Aurora said, feeling a bit embarrassed as the prince and the courtier hovered nearby.

"Oh, dear!" she said, going down the list. "There's so much to do! My dress is ready for a fitting. The flowers need arranging. And the cake—what shall we do about the cake?" There was no time for daydreams any longer. It was time to get down to business.

Play Song 4 Aurora wanted so much to bring her special touch to all the arrangements, but she'd need just a little help. It wasn't

long before the good fairies—Flora, Fauna, and
Merryweather—were on the job. With their magic,
they seemed to be everywhere at once!

The three fairies performed lots of magic—
whipping up a new dress for Aurora, making sure
the food was perfect, and helping to decorate the
courtyard for the party.

♪ **Play Song 5** At last, the day of the party arrived. Prince Phillip surprised Aurora in her dressing room.

"You brought me a garland of flowers from the woods!" exclaimed Aurora. "How perfect!"

"They're to remind you of the time we first met." Prince Phillip smiled as the good fairies made their final adjustments and arranged the garland to their liking.

Just before the party, Princess Aurora stole the prince away for a few minutes. "I have something for you," she said, leading him to the wing of the castle they'd be living in after their wedding.

As they went inside, Prince Phillip looked around happily. "Whoever decorated this has exquisite taste," said the Prince. "It's very similar to my own."

"I decorated it, silly," said Princess Aurora, delighted at the Prince's reaction. "This is my wedding gift to you."

"You know me so well," said the Prince, falling even more in love with Aurora. "We're going to have a happy life here."

"I couldn't agree more," said Aurora.

Play Song 6 At last, they headed off to the party. Aurora and Phillip were delighted to greet so many guests. And everyone agreed that the engagement party was the best they had ever been to. It was everything it should be—classic and elegant, festive and fun.

"May I have this dance?" Prince Phillip and his father, King Hubert, asked Aurora at the exact same time. Princess Aurora's face shone with happiness.

"Go ahead," said King Hubert. "Watching the two of you together makes me happy."

Princess Aurora and Prince Phillip danced 'til all the guests went home. Only the forest animals remained, for they knew that a promise made long ago had been fulfilled in the loveliest way. There was definitely magic in the air!

Play Song 7